JAMES

PERCY

First published in Great Britain 1993 by Buzz Books,
an imprint of Reed International Books Ltd
Michelin House, 81 Fulham Road, London SW3 6RB
and Auckland, Melbourne, Singapore and Toronto

Copyright © 1993 William Heinemann Ltd
All publishing rights: William Heinemann Ltd. All television
and merchandising rights licensed by William Heinemann Ltd
to Britt Allcroft (Thomas) Ltd exclusively, worldwide.

Photographs copyright © 1992 Britt Allcroft (Thomas) Ltd
Photographs by David Mitton and Terry Permane
for Britt Allcroft's production of Thomas the Tank
Engine and Friends

ISBN 1 85591 292 9

Printed in Italy by Olivotto

# MAVIS

buzz books

Mavis is a diesel engine who works for the quarry company, shunting trucks in their sidings. She has six small wheels hidden by sideplates just like Toby's.

Mavis is young and full of her own ideas. She loves rearranging things, too, and began putting Toby's trucks in different places every day.

This made Toby cross. "Trucks," he grumbled, "should be where you want them, when you want them."

"Fiddlesticks," said Mavis and flounced away.

At last Toby lost patience. "I can't waste time playing 'Hunt the Trucks' with you. Take them yourslf."

Mavis was pleased. Taking trucks made her feel important.

9

At the station, Diesel oiled up to her.

"Toby's an old fusspot," she complained.

Diesel sensed trouble and was delighted.

"Toby says only steam engines can manage trucks," continued Mavis.

"How absurd. Depend upon it, Mavis. Anything steam engines can do, we diesels can do better."

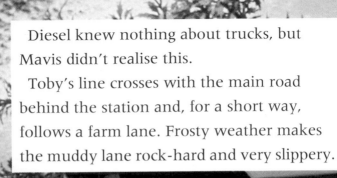

Diesel knew nothing about trucks, but Mavis didn't realise this.

Toby's line crosses with the main road behind the station and, for a short way, follows a farm lane. Frosty weather makes the muddy lane rock-hard and very slippery.

Toby stops before reaching the lane. His fireman halts the traffic at the crossing and then he sets off again. By using the heavy trucks to push him along, he has no trouble with the frosty rails in the lane. It is the only safe thing to do in this kind of weather.

Toby warned Mavis and told her just what to do.

"I can manage, thank you," she replied. "I'm not an old fusspot like you."

The trucks were tired of being pushed around by Mavis.

"It's slippery," they whispered. "Let's push her around instead."

"On, on, on!" they yelled.

Mavis took no notice. Instead she brought
the trucks carefully down the lane and
stopped at the level crossing.

All traffic halted.

"One in the headlamp for fusspot Toby," chortled Mavis.

But Mavis had stopped in the wrong place.

Instead of taking Toby's advice, she had given the trucks the chance they wanted.

"Hold back, hold back!" they cried.

"Grrr-up," ordered Mavis.

The trucks just laughed and her wheels spun helplessly.

Workmen sanded the rails and tried to
dig away the frozen mud, but it was no good.
Everyone was impatient.

"Grrrr-agh!" wailed Mavis.

Toby was in the yard when he heard the news.

"I warned her," he fumed.

"She's young yet," soothed his driver, "and…"

"She can manage her trucks herself," interrupted Toby.

"They're your trucks really," his driver replied. "Mavis is supposed to stay at the quarry. If the Fat Controller finds out …"

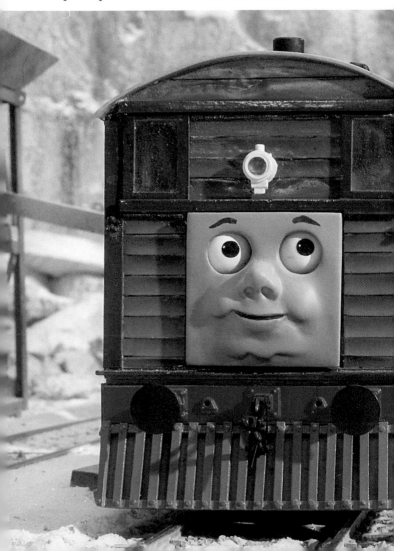

"Hmm, yes," said Toby thoughtfully.

He and his driver agreed that it would be best to help Mavis after all.

An angry farmer was telling Mavis just what she could do with her train!

"Having trouble, Mavis?" chortled Toby. "I am surprised."

"Grrr-osh," said Mavis.

With much puffing and wheel-slip Toby pushed Mavis and the trucks back.

The hard work made his fire burn fiercely and his fireman spread hot cinders to melt the frozen mud.

At last they had finished.

"Goodbye," called Toby. "You'll manage now, I expect."

Mavis didn't answer. She took the trucks to the sheds and scuttled home to the quarry as quickly as she could.

**THOMAS**

**EDWARD**

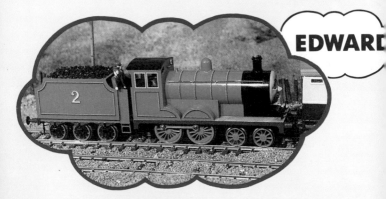

**GORDON**